When Mike's Mother Died

Mai Louise Falsig

Mai Louise Falsig

When Mike's mother died

Children's Book

Images: dreamstime.

ISBN 9788771457421

Publisher: Books on Demand GmbH, Copenhagen, Denmark
Print: Books on Demand GmbH, Norderstedt, Germany

Table of Contents:

Chapter 1
A teasingly lump

Mike was eating his Corn Flakes. All the while, he secretly looked at his mother. It was almost, as she did not sense, that he was present. With a faraway look in her eyes, she sat gazing into nowhere. The smoke was slowly rising in a spiral from the end of the cigarette, she held between her right hand fingers.

Mike knew very well, that she was thinking about the lump which meant that she was mentally absent. She had to go to the Hospital in order to have a lump in her breast examined.

Last night he could not fall asleep. He then happened to overhear his mother and father talking about the lump. His father had several times mentioned that the lump definitely wasn't malignant, that it surely was a mammary gland bearing in mind that she gave birth to his younger sister only a week ago.

It was very…bad? Mike could not imagine how a lump could be bad. Jim in his class was a Devil, because he always teased him about his red hair and pushed him over. Mike happened to attend second grade in Soenderfields's School. He wondered if the lump also was teasing his mother…was a lump able to tease at all.

- Mum! The ash on your cigarette is now almost a yard long!

His mother gave him an ironic smile and put out the cigarette in the ashtray.

- You need not worry Mum. It is definitely not a malignant lump. Mary looked for a short moment at him in surprise. Then she moved to the chair next to his, put her arm around his shoulder and brushed the hair away from his eyes.

- I overheard last night that you and Dad was talking about that lump.

He looked astonished upon his mother, who wiped a tear away from her cheek.

- You have to go to school now Mike. I must be at the Hospital before nine AM…We will talk about it this afternoon.

She rose and left the kitchen. Mike finished his breakfast, picked up his school bag from the floor and hurried out into the Hall. He looked forward to be at school today. The class was to have Danish grammar as a start, and he just loved the Danish language.

Late afternoon his father picked Mike up at the after-school entre. Mike had a lot to tell about an eventful day. He did not noticed, that his father was very unhappy. When they arrived at home, Mike plunked as usual his bag at the floor in the Hall and ran into the kitchen.

- Mum! You never know how much fun we had in…Mum, where are you?

Mike ran into the living room, but he could not see his mother anywhere. His father John entered the living room.

- Mum is still at the Hospital.

Said his father.

Mike immediately felt, that his father was very miserable.

- The lump in her left breast was a malignant tumor…It was…cancer. The doctors have removed her breast, and she will not be home for a week or two.

His father sat down in the sofa. Mike sat down next to him.

- Is it very seriously dad?

John blows his nose in a handkerchief and looked at his son. –

- I do not know Mike. The doctors have removed some lymph nodes too. He told your mum, that they believe, they have succeeded in removing all her cancer…All we can do is praying, that you mother recover her health again.

   Mike rose, ran into his room and slammed the door. He throws himself on the bed and buried his face in the pillow. Why does his mother have to get cancer? Not that he really knew what cancer was. But it was evil, and it has now attacked his mother. Mike new, that his father was very sad. He got up and fell down on his knee by the bedside. He folds his hands.

- Dear God…please make my mother well again. My dad, syounger sister and I cannot do very well do without her.

He once again got to bed. What has started as a fine day has become gray and dreary.

Chapter 2
Nadine's christening

It was today, that his mother would return from the Hospital.   His grandmother was paying them a visit. Together they looked after his younger sister Nadine. She has not yet been christened, but his parents have already decided her name. He had promised his mother and father not to disclose her name. It had to be a big surplice for the rest of the family.

When he now was sitting with his grandma, it was difficult not to tell her anything. Mike knew that he was not good at keeping a secret. However, hes would not tell this particular secret…only to due to his mother. They were playing card, which Mike loved to play. Usually he was winning over his grandma.

The front door opened. Mike throws his cards on the table and ran out into the hall. He throws himself into his mother's arms, while she was just pulling of her coat.

- Mike dear me. I have just been away for a couple of weeks. Did you miss me that much?...Often I have attended a course with you ignoring the fact that I wasn't home.

Mike let go his Mother, which enabled her to take of her coat.

- How are you doing mum? Are you completely well?
Mary took his hand and they walked into the kitchen where she hugged his grandma. She turned towards Mike.
- I certainly take it for granted. As you know, your mother is a fighter.
Mike danced at the kitchen floor, all the while he was drumming at the kitchen cabinets with his hands.
- My mom is well…my mom is well!
Mikes grandma Mina cleaned up the dining table in the kitchen. - We passed the time playing cards…I...
Her voice broke without completing the sentence.
- I have made coffee. Baby sister has been sleeping, since John went to pick you up Mary.
She sighed.
- I have been at the bakery…I'll lay the table.
Mary gave her mother a grateful smile.
- You are so kind mother…I will look after baby sister. I have to nurse her. My breast is about to burst.
Mike looked at his mom, and he could see, that her left side was completely flat without any curve, where her breast  used to be. If her right breast burst too, his mom would have no boobs at all.   How where Nadine then able to have any food? Did his mom have enough milk at all, with only one breast? Mike got quite scared. Would Nadine now starve to death? He went

12

into the livingroom, where his mother sat in a small sofa breastfeedingShe wore a wig but Mike he preferred the bandana. There was lit in the fireplace. It comforted, for the winter for was approaching fast Mike sat down in the sofa he did not really know how to tell his mother, what was on his mind.

- Mom…do you think, that you have enough milk to baby sister, in the remaining breast?

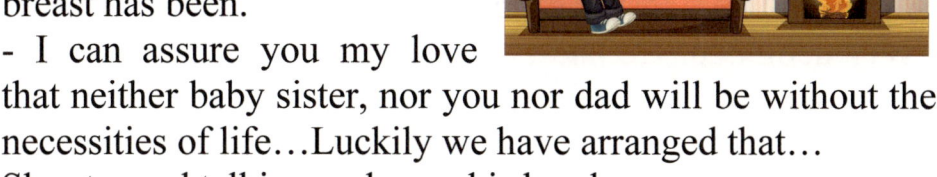

He could clearly see the white bandage, where her other breast has been.

- I can assure you my love that neither baby sister, nor you nor dad will be without the necessities of life…Luckily we have arranged that…

She stopped talking and gave his hand a squeeze.

- You have arranged what mom?

Mary let go his hand and helped Nadine finding the nipple once more.

- Nothing Mike. You just pop out and help grandma lay the coffee table. I will soon be around with Nadine.

Mike's grandma had made hot cocoa and whip-ped cream to Mike. But why not celebrate. His mother has returned healthy from the hospital. The past days anxiety for her health was gone, and inwardly he thanked God, because he had heard his prayers.

Soon his mother came out into the kitchen, and together they had a cosy time with cookies, that his grandma has bought. It was almost as it was somebody's birthday. They hardly ever were together at a coffee table at the afternoon. Very soon, they talked about Nadine's christening, and whether his mother would be fit for such a party. His mom laughed and ensured his grandma, that she soon would be as fit as a white-tailed eagle. How his mother knew, what is was like to be a white-tailed eagle, was a mystery to Mike. She had to know, since she always said so.

As the days goes by, Mike even less thought about his mothers illness. Nadine was to be christened, and Mike was very delighted. He had never been to a christening before. Silly me...he had of cause been to his own christening. However, he could not remember anything at all, due to his young age at that time.

Nadine was dresses in her fine christening gown, and now they were driving in the car on their way to the church. After the christening they were to drive to the town's old village hall to have diner. His parents had ordered icecream for dessert, and icecream was Mike's favorite food.

The preast baled water over Nadine's head, while she screamed at the top of her voice.

Mike was convinced, that she was screaming, because the water was very cold. They might as well heat the water just a little bit prior putting it in the font. He smiled at his grandma, who brushed a tear away from her cheek. She was always crying…not because she was sad. She also cried, when she was happy, she once has told him.

It was Rikke, Mike's aunt, who carried his baby sister. She was to be Nadine's godmother. Mike could not understand how Rikke at the same time was his aunt and Nadine's (Which means everybody's) God's mother. Was she Jesus' stepmother too? Did she really saw his crucifixtion? Mike had always been told that Rikke was born in 1980; but that couldn't be true. She must be over 2014 years old! Mike was all questions but no answers. He maybe one day should ask her if it was how it was. And how God looked like. Dear me! Why had he not thought about this sooner? Rikke could tell God, next time she meets him, that his mother never should be sick any more.

Mike looked at all the fine presents, which Nadine has received. It was waterproof, that she would be disappointed, when she saw all the clothes, cups, knives and forks lying on the table. She had received very little toys. Christmas and birthdays were much better. Them one got much better presents.

They sat down at the table. Both his father and an uncle delivered a speech. They were singing two songs, and Mike was by now fed up with all these breaks. Mike had to put down his fork and knife and be quiet, while he was in the middle of his delicious meal. It was difficult to sit quiet in a chair for such a long time. His meal would soon become quite cold. It would have been much better, if they have served a plate with nice cold buttermilk with a touch of lemon and a lot of crunch instead of warm roasted veal. Then it would not matter with all these breaks.

The veal finally was over and done, and the dessert was served. They were about to have ice cream gateau, and Mike just loved ice cream.

He was so satiated, that he almost did not have the energy to move his legs. He should maybe not have eaten the third serving of ice cream.

Mikes mother told him, that he now had to have his photograph taken, while he was sitting with Nadine. His mom and dad always took a bundle photos every time they had a party. Why take pictures, when they most of the time just were put away in a computer or books afterwards. They had also hired a professional photographer, who should make a DVD movie of Nadine's baptism. He went around and bullied everyone present. When Mike sat down with Nadine he cried that Mike was sitting at her christening robe.

Mike didn't care. He gave her a smile and she returned his smile. Mike could not help being a little bit proud. Nadine was guaranteed the most wonderfull baby sister in the world.

When they finally got home safe and happy, they all agreed, that it had been a nice party. Mike was sure, that Nadine agreed too, however she was yet unable to express her opinion. Mike put on his nightclothes at once and brushed his teeth. When he was in his bed under the duvet, he gave Nadine's christening a happy thought. He by now luckily had forgotten that his mother had been ill.

Chapter 3
The chemotherapy.

Since Nadine had been christened, a couple of months have now past away. His mother's illness had once more deteriorated. His parents therefore went to the hospital today. Mike had told her, that she by guarantee has cached the flue. She had smiled at him and gently stroked his hair saying that he probably was right.

Mike was in his room playing with his action man. After a couple of minutes, he put the doll on its place on the shelf. He did not really want to play. His thought about his mom's illness. He kept turning it over in his mind. If only she was not sick for real.

The door to his room opened and his grandma entered the room. – Do you feel like a game of card?

Mike shrugs his shoulders. He did not feel for doing anything, nevertheless if he played a game of card with his grandma. He would not think so much about his mom.

Mike's grandmother had warmed some buns in the oven. He was soon so wrapped up in the game and the yummy buns that he forgot to be sad.

His dad returned home late afternoon. When Mike heard the sound from the front doors hinge, he ran into the hall to meet him. He looked astonished at his dad.

- Where is mom?

John took Mike in his arms.

- Your mother is still at the hospital.

Mike looked frightened at his dad. He could se, how sad he was. - Is mum sick once more?

Mike's dad nodded his head.

- The doctors removed what you call lymph nodes…Your mother has still cancer…It has attacked a big part of her body.

Mike fought back his tears.

- Mom is not going to die…is she? She will once more recover and get well…wont she?

Mike's dad gave him a big hug and looked very sad at Mike's grandmother.

- Sure!...Mom is going to be okay…It is not very serious. All she has to do is to take some medicine called chemotherapy. She had a cure when they had removed her breast; but now she is going to have the strongest chemotherapy, they have. Your mom then will be as good as a newborn baby.

He placed Mike on the floor and together they went out into the kitchen. It suddenly did not matter playing card or eating warn soft rolls. His mother was ill once more.

His dad picked Mike up a fortnight later at the after-school centre. When he got home his mom had returned home from the hospital. She was very tired and as white as a sheet. Mike got surprised, when he saw her; but happy to see her home again.

- Mom! Are you okay now?

He ran to her and gave his mom a big hug. She was lying on the sofa with a plaid over her legs.

- No…not yet…but I will be. First, I have to undergo this chemotherapy.

Mike sat down on the sofa next to his mother.

- Why are you so pale mum?

She gave him a wry smile.

- It is the chemotherapy. It is obviously not good for me.

She had barely said her last word, when she rapidly tugged the plaid away from her legs and got up from the sofa. Mike fell down at the floor with a big thud and his mother ran at full speed out into the bathroom. Mike could hear her vomit. He hurried out into the bathroom, where his dad was holding his arm around his mother.

- Are you sick mom?

She washed her face in cold water from the washbasin and wiped her face and hands with a towel.

- I am much better now.

Mike was mad at the hospital. Why did they give his mother chemotherapy? Everybody knew that chemicals were not healthy. He had heard it so often in the television. That was the reason why his parents always bought organic meat, vegetables and other everyday necessities. The doctors ought to provide his mother with organic therapy instead. This would be much better for her. He would tell her, when she once more entered the living room.

Mary entered the living room carrying Nadine. She sat down in the sofa and started to feed her with a nursing bottle. Mike watched with great interest, while Nadine was drinking the milk eagerly.

- Why don't you breast feed Nadine anymore?

Mike was curious and wanted to know why. He fondled her small fingers.

- Mike, I do not believe, it is the right thing to do. Having chemotherapy, I do not know if all these toxic substance will harm her. That's why I don't.

Mike frown his brows. They were giving his mom not just chemicals. It was pure poison. No wonder she was ill. Poison would kill you; he knew that. But she maybe needed to be so ill in order to be well?

As the days went by his mum started to loose more and more of her hair. Mike sensed that she did not like it at all. Gradually she started wearing a headscarf. Mike had to admit, that she looked odd without hair on her head.

They were sitting together at the dining table in the kitchen.

She was helping him reading a page in his English schoolbook. It was his homework for tomorrow.

Mike was by now a very good reader although he only was nine years old. His mom had a dayoff. She was a dentist and she had a dentist clinic together with another woman. However, she was so queasy when she had had chemotherapy that she preferred to stay at home. Mike felt sorry for his mom, but he was on the other hand happy not had to join the after-school center.

- Will you never grow hair on your head again?

Mike stopped reading from the book and looked upon his mom. She smiled at him.

- I sure will honey. When I am done with the chemotherapy, it had better start growing, or I will be mad.

Mike closed his book and put it into his school bag.

- Mom, in a way it is maybe fine, that you do not have any hair. You always grumble about your hair never sit the way you want it to do. Furthermore, you do not have to spend all that money at the hairdresser dyeing your hair.

Mary wrinkled her eyebrows and slapped him gentle on the shoulder.

- You look as always so convenient to everything ... I think that I, after all, would rather have my hair.

Mike got up and pushed the chair into its place at the table.

- You look much better too with your hair mom.

He went silent and bid his lips. Could be that he now had made his mother sad. He gave her a big hug.

- I have to say, that you are very smart with all these beautiful scarves too.

He picked up his school bag from the floor and ran into his room.

Mary turned off the light over the dining table in the kitchen and went out in the hallway.

- I am taking a litte power nap on the couch Mike. If you are going to visit Frank, then you should be home by half past five, because we are eating early tonight.

Mike biked over to Frank, who only lived a few houses further along the road. Frank was his best playmate, and they sat beside each other at school. He put his bike up against the wall just beside the door to the utility room and rang the doorbell. Frank's mother opened the door.
- Oh, is it you Mike? Go on ... Frank is sitting in the living room. He is watching the television.
Mike ran into the room. The adults were very strange. Why did she ask, whether it was he, who stood in the doorway? She could probably very well see it was he.

Frank slapped his hand down into the sofa cushion beside him. - Hurry on Mike ... I am about to see "Pirates of the Carabian" on DVD ... it is a very good movie you will enjoy it. I might start the movie all over if you want to see the whole movie.
Mike nodded his head and sat on the couch while Frank fumbled with the remote control.

Franks mother came into the living room. She placed two canned cola and a basket full of chips on the table.
- I thought that you might need this seeing the movie.
They started immediately to empty the content in the basket. Frank's mother was just super. They were soon

wrapped up in the film, and Mike had forgotten all about his mother and her scarves around her head.

Chapter 4
Christmas Eve

It was December 24 and Mike was so excited that he had almost stomachache. He was fortunate that there was so much on television, or else he did not know how he would have suvieved the very long day. He particularly liked to watch Disney's Christmas Show, which he annually sees together with his mum and dad.

Nadine sat in her sloping chair on the floor, but how much fun she she had seeing Snow White, he did not know. Time dragged away. Mike looked at the grandfather clock; it was not more than five. It would last more than an hour, befor they were going to dine. He looked dreamy at the Christmas tree that stood in the middle of the floor in all its glory. The electric lights from the chain shone with my colourt on tinsel and all the balls.

They had a nice Christmas tree not as ornate as with Mickey Mouse and Pluto. He looked at all packcore that went right up to the lower branches. His father had even been forced to cut some branches, in order to make room for all gifts. Every year, his father said that this year would be a discount christmas finish with all the numerous and expensive gifts. As far as Mike could see, there were more gifts this year than there had ever been. His grandmother came into the room, she celebrated Christmas with them every year. Mike's grandparents celebrated Christmas with them every other year. This year they were at his uncle Peter.

- Grandma do you bother break any nuts to me?

Mike had tried; but it was impossible to crack the nuts. He hasn't got that kind of power yet. His grandmother picked the nutcracker up from the table.

- Of course, Mike ... in the meantime you can then fill the dish with Christmas candy? It's all ready in the kitchen.

Christmas candies! Mike jumped down on the floor and ran into the kitchen. On the table stood all the boxes filled with the sweetest delights. Everything was homemade. He had helped his mother and father to do it all.

The dinner was roast goose, and Mike just loved the crispy skin. As usual, he also found an almond in his portion of rice a la mande. His almond gift was a new CD. It was just before he forgot all about dancing around the Christmas tree, he was so anxious to hear the music in his room.

After they had gone through the whole song booklet. (Mike thought at least they were), the gifts were handed around to everybody. As always, all the gifts were handed out, before one individually began opening his or hers package. Mike simply got everything he wanted, and he beamed tracery with the lights on the Christmas tree. Now it was his mother's turn. Mike looked excited at her, when she wrapped the presents out. Why didn't she soon take gift from him? Now she had hold of it, he held his breath as she lifted out the parrot in plush. Mike hurried over to his mother.

- It can be put on the shoulder mother ... so it's simply a crutch to imitate him pirate Long John Silver from

"Treasure Island" ...Now you can always go with a pirate scarf around her head.

His mother slapped him.

- You're a teaser!

She took him to her and gave him a hug.

- Thank you for the gift Mike.

He wrapped his arms around her mother.

- It's not all you get mom ... I'm also a gift from Dad.

She let go of him and smiled.

- What, however, I get spoiled this year. I wonder what my clients would say if I stood and orderly teeth at them with a parrot on my shoulder?

The rest of the evening passed all too quickly away. Mike sighed. Now there was a whole year until it again was Christmas Eve. In the morning he would go to Frank, to tell him about his many gifts.

Chapter 5
Cupid's arrows

Mike's mother was finished with the chemotherapy and she was starting to feel much better. Mike could also tell that she was happier than she had been a long time. Her good mood infected both Mike and his father, so it was not long until they no longer spoke of the cancer. Mike also remembered to thank God every night when he prayed evening prayer. Maybe he should say to his aunt Rikke, that she should thank him the next time she saw him.

Mary's hair was once again started to grow, and she had a few millimeters short hair covering her head. One morning, when they were busy getting out the door, Mary rummaged through her bag.

- Where's my comb, has anyone seen my comb?

Mike and his father had looked at her with wondering eyes, then they all had laughed bursting in tears. His mother soon realized that it was not yet necessary that she had her comb with her at work. Mike thought that she looked cool. He had also told her that she looked like a tuff American Navy Seal, for he had just seen an action movie where they were heroes or at least one Ranger. She had laughed and told him that there certainly wasn't much hunter in her. The only bull that she previously had to lie down was her husband. Mike was not fully aware of the meaning in hers saying. But it was fun, he was not in doubt. His father had certainly

laughed when his mother said it. It rummaged inside his head. Was there something about that when you lay down an animal it meant that you shot it? He grabbed his mother by the shirt.
- Mom what did you use when you shot dadv? She smiled. Cupid's arrows I suppose. She squatted.
- You see Mike, when that woman gets hold of a man, so they say that you have got him. It simply means that the woman has been made him fall in love with one. Mike glanced in wonder at his mother. - Where do you get these Cupid's arrows? There is a girl attention in school, which I'm quite excited about. Mary laughed.
- You have shown no arrows ... with your great charm, just to scratch on.

She quickly got her coat and grabbed Mike's school bag.
- We're late to school if we do not hurry up young man.
Mike took his winter jacket on and put his feet into the shoes.
- Are you also attending school, since you said we?
She laughed and gave him a light slap on his head.
- Yes, I will ... you were not aware that your mom again are a student? Be careful that I do not throw snowballs at you at recess. By the way you loosen your shoes before putting them on.
She opened the door and walked out to the car. Mike was happy to get his "old" healthy mother again.

When they passed the house where Frank lived, Frank was walking out to the car with his mother. Mary stopped the BMW and rolled down the window in the front passenger door.

- We may as well take Frank with us. Yhis will save your the trip to the school. Before Frank's mother could answer, Frank had sat in the back seat of the BMW next to Mike. They soon fell into conversation, and before long they reached the school. The snowball fight already was underway in the schoolyard, and they vanished into the courtyard with a short "Goodbye".

Chapter 6
The cancer arises once again its arrival

Just as they had come back into the daily routine, Mike's mother began to feel bad. She started to get tired faster, and her mood was not the best.

One day she slipped in the small rug at home in the hall and fell so awkwardly that she fractured femur. She went to the hospital where they kept her for some studies. Mike could not understand why they do not just pack her into the plaster so they could get her back home.

After a few days they took again to the hospital to visit Mike's mother. The doctor told them that his mother's cancer once again marched forward. It had spread to the bones. It was thus that her femur had broken so easily. Mike did not like to be in the hospital. It smelled of death and disease. He did not like that his mother was lying with all the the intravenous needles into her body. She was in a room with two other ladies. They lay with empty eyes and waere quite pale and had a translucent skin.

When his mother had been in hospital for more than two weeks, she was again allowed to come home. She was started on yet another very strong chemotherapy, and soon she lost all her hair again. She was so tired and sick because of the cure that she didn't bother to put the scarf on his head every morning. She borrowed therefore a cap of Mike, she used instead of the scarf. He had tried to persuade her to turn it upside down on her head, because he thought that she would look cooler.

Her bones were soon so fragile that she could no longer walk, so they had to drive her around in a wheelchair. They borrowed a bed at the hospital. It was electric and you could raise and lower it. It was placed in the living room, as it was impossible for his mother to come upstairs.

The cure with the strong medicine was replaced by a milder cure, that Mike's mother could continue to get a long time. But after a short period the effect began to wane, and his father told me that the doctors had said that they could not do more for his mother. That night Mike had been crying all night long. He was thinking about the old and sick Mrs. Jones down at number 25. She was over 85 years old. He knew of course that you do not wish that other people should die. But why couldn't she die instead of his mother? He also heard someone whisper that death was the best thing that could happen to his mother, when you take her illness into account. But death was not the best thing that could happen to someone like a little 9 year old boy, who needs his mother.

His mother was soon so ill that she needed help with everything. A nurse and a social- & health worker came several times a day, and his mother was mostly just in bed with her eyes closed. The doctors had suggested that she again had to be hospitalized; but his mother had protested.

She wanted to die at home in familiar surroundings, surrounded by her family. Mike's grandmother moved in with them. She looked after his mother was cooking and washing clothes. She picked him up at school, too; but he would rather have been picked up by his mother.

Mike's mother died, early sunday afternoon, while the nurse was on a routine visit. His father, aunt Rikke and his grandmother did not think it was something for a little boy to attend. He had therefore been sent to his room with his cousin Donald, where they sat and watched TV. Mike would much rather have been sitting in the dining room, holding his mother's hand. He could not concentrate on the movie, he kept thinking of his mother. When the film was nearly finished, Mike's father entered the room and told him that his mother had died. Mike could not say anything he just stared blankly into the empty space. The tears pressed forward; but he could not cry. He got up from the bed and hugged his father. His father picked him up in her arms, gave him a hug and then went into the dining room. Mike noted that one window was open, and he looked questioningly at his father, who followed Mike's gaze.
- The nurse who has opened the window ... it was to enable your mother's soul to fly out.

He sat Mike down on the floor beside the coffin. Mike was a little angry when he heard his father's words. It would have been much better if his mother's soul had been in the house with them, inside his mom. He looked at his mother, who lay peacefully in her bed. Mike could see that her face was no longer twisted in pain. Yet he was angry with God, who had allowed his mother to die. That could only mean that God hadn't heard him at all. He had asked for his mother getting well, that she would not die. Maybe God had too much to do. He had to do a million things all around the world. Maybe that's why he hadn't heard Mike's prayers. Mike's dad called the emergency central, who would send a doctor as soon as possible to look for safe signs of death and issue a death certificate.

The rest of the afternoon went Mike as if in a daze. It could not be that his mother had died. She was guaranteed just sleeping. In a moment she would open her eyes and tell them that
it had just been a bad joke.

Chapter 7
A last Goodby

Mike tried to watch the cartoon on television; but his thoughts were constantly about the things that are currently going on in the bedroom. His mother had died yesterday afternoon, and ask the man was with his aunt and grandmother Rikke by dressing his mother well on and put her in the coffin. His father sat with him in the living room, and he had a distant look in his eyes. Mike could see that he was not so much television.

- Dad, are you thinking also of the mother?

His father nodded and looked at him with sad eyes.

- Yes, of course I can not help Mike ... she has not even been dead a day and I already miss her so much. Mike knew well what he meant, he wanted namely also that his mother was sitting next to this guy on the couch so he could snuggle in to her.

His grandmother came into the room, and Mike could see that her eyes were moist.

- Now we are done ... I think that you better say goodbye to your mom before the undertaker puts the lid on the coffin.

She walked over and patted Mike on the cheek.

- Don't you want to say goodbye to your mother Mike?

Mike thought that it would have been better if they had allowed him to be present when his mother died so he could have said goodbye to her there. But it seemed that his father and grandmother didn't want him to. He turned off the TV and went with hand in hand with his father into the dining room. His mother was looking fine in the coffin dressed in her nicest set. His father had given his mom her beloved laptop. He told Mike that she couldn't do whitout in heaven. It looked as if she just lay sleeping. Mike approached the coffin and stroked his mother gently on the cheek. He wanted to say goodbye to her; but a lump in his throat caused that he could not utter a sound. Tears rolled Instead silently down his cheeks. His father put his arm around his shoulder. Aunt Rikke sat at the dining table, and Mike could see that she had been crying. He didn't need to be ashamed of his tears. It was okay to be great and still be sad.

Mike considered the coffin, which had some beautiful flowering vines on the side. Suddenly he could see that something was wrong. He tore his father by the shirt.
- There are no air holes in the coffin, how could his mother breathe, if she wakes up again?
His aunt had in fact explained to him yesterday that the doctor had to examine his mother for sure signs of death to be sure that she really was dead and did not appear to be dead. The doctor would then issue a death certificate. Maybe she was still just appearing to be dead? Then it would be terrible if she woke up unable to breathe. His father looked a little confused, and then came an

explanatory expression on his face. He looked at the mortuary.

- Mother is dead Mike ... it's almost unbearable, I know. But we must accept that it is over now.

Mike thought, so it creaked. He had to do something right now? Now he knew it ~ his mother's cell phone. He ran into the living room, turned on the phone and checked that it was charged, and then he again went into the dining room.

- Goodbye mother.

Mike's tears trickled down upon the cheek of his mother. He put the cell phone in her hand, then without either his father or the undertaker saw it, he coaxed the mobile phone under her pillow.

- The mobile phone is under your pillow mother.

He whispered softly.

- If you now wake up again.

He got up and took his father's hand. His father stroked his hair affectionately, nodding to the undertaker. The undertaker and his assistant then listed the lid on the coffin. Tomorrow should the coffin with Mike's mother be transported out of something called the chapel in the cemetery? There was the coffin to be until she was to be buried on Saturday.

The rest of the day was the coffin with his mother in the dining room in a last goodbye.
Mike acknowledged seeing the coffin through the door of the hall was a beautiful and peaceful sight.

Chapter 8
The funeral

There was a strange atmosphere in the house, everyone was walking around and waited for the time passing nine o'clock, so they could get off to the chapel. Mike's grandmother looked for the tenth time in the mirror in the hall looking at the scarf she had around her neck. His father sat quietly in his chair, wringing his hands, which he had in his lap. Mike was glad that it wasn't every day they attend a funeral because he could not remember when everyone had been so sad.

His father looked at his watch and rose from the chair. Now we'd better get there. Please take your coat on Mike? I'll come with Nadine. Mike went out into the hall, where he nearly tumbled into his grandmother, who once again stood in front of the mirror - You do not have to pay more on your hairstyle or your scarf grandmother, I think you look great. She smiled at him and bent down to give him a hug.

They drove off in the car and arrived at no time at the chapel. Mike could see that most of the family had turned up. When they came into the chapel, the coffin with his mother stood in the middle of the room. It was adorned with a magnificent funeral bouquet, which contained only yellow roses. The yellow rose had been his mother's favorite flower. In the chapel the undertaker said a few words, and they sang two songs including "Always cheerful as you go." {in danish: Altid frejdig når du går} Mike tried to hold back the crying; but it was not easy when almost all of them were in tears.

Both Mike's father, his uncles, his mother's brother Henning and his aunts carried the coffin. Mike had plagued his father if he could not be allowed to carry too. But his father thought that the coffin was probably too heavy for him, so he had denied, which had disappointed Mike a lot. Why couldn't his father understand how much it had meant to him to carry the coffin as well?

When the coffin had come into the hearse, a word that Mike did not like, they drove in convoy behind the same hearse to the church. Mike noticed that some of the people they passed on the road, stopped and saluted as they drove past. Mike was astonished, how could they know that it was his mother who was lying in the coffin?

As they carried the coffin into the church, the entire middle floor was filled with wreaths and bouquets. Mike had never seen so many flowers at once before. The whole church was filled. He had no idea that his mother knew so many people. They had certainly never been on a visit at their home.

The priest gave a speech to his mother, and they sang some hymns; but Mike noticed that neither his father nor his grandmother sang. His father just sat and stared blankly toward the coffin, and his grandmother she sat all the time and wiped his eyes with a handkerchief.

Mike had taken his own mobile phone and put it on silent if his mum woke up and could not understand why she was lying down in a coffin, or the sound of all the people who sang. So she could take his phone and call them. They would all be happy if she suddenly rang. Mike put his hand into his jacket pocket, in case the phone vibrated. If his mom called he was ready to answer.

As the ceremony in the church was finished they carried the coffin out of the cemetery, out to the grave which was a big hole, as his mother had to lie down in. The priest threw earth on the coffin with a small shovel as he muttered the words: "From ashes you have come to dust you shall return, and the earth will again occur. "Mike gave special attention to the last word, even the priest was not sure that his mother was dead. He just said that she again had to get up from the ground.

They had each been given a yellow rose as they one by one went to the grave and threw the rose down on top of the coffin. Mike almost thought it was a shame to throw them into the hole when the coffin was covered with soil there was no one who could see the beautiful flowers.

After the funeral, they drove into the village hall, where they a year before had kept his little sister Nadine's christening. At that time there had been a different cheerful mood. Mike could well understand that noone laughed there was certainly nothing to laugh at. His father had ordered dinner and coffee, and the room was filled by families and many of his parents' friends. Although it was not a happy event, there was still more who smiled when his father told of his mother's many little quirks. Among other things, her weakness for shoes she owned at least a hundred pairs. Mike's father believed that the shoe store in the city would probably go bankrupt, now his mother was dead.

When they again came home, said Mike's father warm thank you to her grandmother's offer to stay overnight. Mike watched TV and tried to help but think of his mother; but he still could not help but be a little disappointed that she had not yet called.

Chapter 9
The answering machine

When he came into the room, Mike discovered that the little red light on the phone was turned on. This meant that someone had left a message on the answering machine. Maybe it was his mother who had called while his father was at work and he even at school. Mike pulled the key message; but sadly it was only his aunt Rikke, who had called.

His mother was probably already in heaven, and that was by no means certain that the signals from the cell phone could reach the Earth completely from up there. But if she was still in the ground inside the coffin, there might be a chance.

Mike knelt down on the chair and looked out the window. The rain got into the ropes, it was a terrible storm. His father had mentioned it as torrential rain and the road at the school had also been covered by 20 centimeters of water. Mike hoped his mother was now in heaven. If she lay down in the coffin, she was guaranteed to drown now. Mike interrupted his own train of thought. What a stupidity his mother was dead and you could not die twice, so she was guaranteed not to drown. As far as he knew, it was only cats had nine lives.

Mike's father came into the room.
- What do you think of hamburgers tonight with onions?

Mike jumped off the chair and ran to his father.

- We might have; but Aunt Rikke has called and invited us to veal roast ... I have heard her message on the answering machine ... Please dad?

Not that Mike better liked Roast veal instead of beef patties; but there was so empty with only him, Nadine and his father at the table. At Rikke there was more life in rags. Mike knew that he was going to get used to, that they were only three people in the house; but need it to be right now?

Mike had understood that his mother died of cancer; but still nagged a little doubt his heart. His mother had sometimes said that she was tired of him, maybe she had not been so tired of him that she had decided to die. Maybe it was really his fault that she died?

Every time Mike had asked her how she felt, she replied: "Very well." She would then have guessed that she was not feeling well, that she was dying. Why had she or his father not said anything about it so he could get used to the idea? Although it probably was hard to get used to someone you love dearly was going to die. And on the other hand ... you couldn't at all get used to something like that? He had never gotten used to the vaccinations at the doctor, even though he knew well in advance that he was going up and stuck.

His father hung up.

- Now I'll change Nadine, we'll take over to Rikke. Grandmother comes too, so we are a whole company.

Mike went with his father to the bathroom, where he laid Nadine up on the changing table. It was not because he was particularly interested in the smell; but right now he just felt like that all three would be together. Nadine chatted and smiled, so it was a pleasure. She had not actually allowed being so happy, now she had lost her mother. But maybe she was so small that she did not know that her mother was dead. When his father had finished changing Nadine, they hurried into the garment and drove over to Rikke.

Chapter 10
Silence

There was almost gone half an hour of the Danish lesson. Danish used to be Mike's best subjects; but today the time went very slowly. It was now nearly two weeks since his mother had died, and neither teachers nor his classmates had discussed it with a single word. They had not asked how he was, or how it went at home. He wanted that they spoke to him, as they used to do instead of packing him up in cotton wool. It seems like Mike was a crazy boy. His mother was not the death of a contagious disease, so he was not affected in any way, why did they moved around him as the cat around the cream?

The only one who had asked a little about how he was doing, was Frank; but he had hardly had time to wait for a response. It was of course terrible when someone's parents died; but why couldn't his mates nevertheless talk about it. His father had told him one day shortly after his mother's funeral: "The only thing people were sure in this world it was that they one day would die." Still, it was almost a taboo subject ... something you did not talk about. Now when you certain were going to die. Mike thought that it was strange that no one talked about it. He certainly had a great need to talk about his feelings and thoughts about his mother's death. One day when he in the school yard stood with Rie, Amalie and Niels, he had been trying to talk about the subject; but they were just so stupid. Amalie had said that she as sadly had lost her great-grandmother, and that it not had been so bad. And thus was the debate on the subject completed. Couldn't she get into her head that it was completely different to lose one's own mother?

Finally, the Danish lesson passed. Mike simply could not keep his mind clear in the classroom. His mind circled still too much about his mother. She was there no more to help him with his homework. She had always done. Now his father helped him every night after dinner. But at first Mike had little desire to do homework so late every night, and secondly, his father didn't possess the same angelic patience as his mother had. Mike walked over to himself and sat on a bench in a corner of the schoolyard. He did no more part in the others crazy play.

When he had been in no more than a few minutes a

blonde girl sat down beside him.
- Hello! My name is Majken, going to the fourth grade.
Mike looked at her. He did have seen her before; but he did not know her name Majken. What would she be him? It was rare that someone

from the larger classes would deal with the smaller children.

- Didn't you just loose your mother?

Continued the girl.

- I have lost my father three months ago, so if you want to talk about whatever you want ... go ahead. I missed for someone to talk to when my father died. I have bougt this box of chocolate to you.

- Why?

Mike looked surprised her, and scraped with the shoe into the asphalt.

- Oh! I really do not know ... there is not really anything to talk about and I'm very fond of chocolate when im sad. Maybe you like the same kind of comfort? The shape of a hart…My dad used to say before he died. "If you need to process your grief then you will need to open your heart."

Mike took the box of chokolates.

- He was right ... you know ... and ... thanks a lot.

Mike got up from the bench.

- I miss my dad still crazy, said Majken quiet.

Mike looked at her and saw that she meant every word she said. Imagine that you could miss a parent after three whole months!

I immediately phoned in to a hour. Majken got up too.

- We can talk a little further when we have another break.

xMike nodded.

- Thank you.

Majken turned around.

- For what?

  She does not think they should make a big deal out of a box of chocolates.

- Because you wanted to talk to me about it!

She gave him a wry smile.

- I have as much need to talk about it as you have.

- Also for the box.

- You're welcome.

Majken rounded the corner at the school's main building, and she was soon out of sight.

Chapter 11
Wednesdays

Mike's grandmother unlocked the door, and he ran ahead of her into the hallway. He could immediately tell that the whole house smelled of freshly baked pate. He was very fond of Wednesday; it was this special day when his grandmother fetched him in the school's playgroup, so he came home early. His father always had so many meetings on Wednesday that was why she fetched him.

- You've baked pâté grandmother!
She laughed and put his shoes neatly along the wall. He had, as usual, kicked them off out of the middle of the floor in the hallway.

- I certainly have ... and bought fresh bread. I'm wondering if the two of us would not enjoy ourselves with a couple of warm bread with liver pâte and a glass of milk.
Mike nodded in agreement and ran into the kitchen, where the table was already covered. Wednesday was all just matter. His grandmother had always something delicious prepared for him.

While they silently sat and ate, Mike began to think of his mother. It was her liver pâte, which they ate. She had in

50

fact managed to make a great deal before she died. I wish she had not died. He missed her so much. A little treacherous tear began to trickle out of the corner of his right eye. Mike wiped the tear away with the back of his hand and stared blankly into the air.

- Are you thinking about your mother Mike?

Her grandmother's voice brought him back to reality. He nodded without looking at her. She put her hand over his, which was on the table.

- It's always hard to lose one of your loved ones ... I know how hard it is to get over the loss ... I miss her too ... so much ... and even though it is many years since your grandfather died I still miss him.

Mike took his hand away and got up quickly from the table. He ran into his room and slammed the door behind him, while the tears trickled out. He lay down on the bed and grabbed his plush kangaroo, which his mother had bought for him at the time they had been on holiday in Australia. After a few minutes he got up and walked over to his desk. Mike opened the box and took a piece of heart-shaped filled chocolate... Uuhhmm! He sent Majken a kind thought, She was very sweet {*a **Jutland** understatement to say when she is incredibly sweet and desirable*}. Mike was looking forward to see her again.

Chapter 12
You should always call a spade a spade

Why did adults all these words about death? He had not lost his mother, if you lose something, then you have a hope that it would be found, so you can get it again. Mike sighed. He had not lost his mother. He knew where her grave was. He never got his mother again.
- To recover from his loss!
Mike almost sneered the words out. His father was CFO of a large corporation, and if it had "incurred losses" in a trade, it was possible to cover it in by other trades, so much did he.
He could not get his mother covered. There would never be someone who could replace her. His mother was dead ... gone ... all gone. It surprised him that he had not heard either his father or his mother throughout the course of the disease say the word "death." His father had not said: Death ... without wrapping it. Were they afraid to say the word? Or, they believed that their many rewrites of the word made it glide down ... seem less real? Mike did not understand.
His aunt Rikke had said that God had called her home. But it could not be true. His mother's home was with his father, Nadine and himself. She had no right to say that his mother was at home with God. She was godmother, so she thought she knew it; but maybe that was because she was a dentist, she was on a "home visit?" His mother should perhaps fix

God's teeth. He slapped angrily the right palm down on the desk top. If that was the cause of his mother's death, God was damn tacky. A lot of dentists were probably died over the past several years. If God had bad teeth, he could have chosen one of them. It was totally unnecessary to fetch his mother. Mike hugged her kangaroo and thought of his mother. He did not notice that the kangaroo was becoming quite wet because of his many tears.

Chapter 13
The birthday

Mike had come home from camp by bus yesterday afternoon. His father picked him up at the school and it had almost been a stab in the heart of Mike when he saw some of the other kids get into the car with their mother. It was not because he did not love his father; but he just missed his mother so much.

Today was Mike's birthday, he turned eleven years. He hadn't celebrated his tenth birthday as it was shortly after his mother's death. At the breakfast table were both a gift from aunt, father and Nadine. Mike wrapped the presents out. From his father was an action game for the computer. It used to be his mother's stationary computer: but was moved into his room after her death. Mike was happy to play on the computer; but he would rather that his mother still lived. From grandmother was a new watch, his old clock had gone to pieces, and Nadine gave him a new shirt. He said thanks for the gifts and gave them all a big hug. Nadine sat in his high chair. She was not particularly interested in a hug. She would rather strike the Corn Flakes with her spoon.

When he came home from school, the whole house will be filled with guests. Mike had invited al his classmates they were having soft drinks, birthday cake and hamburgers. His cousin Donald also came and his aunt

Rikke had promised to help. Mike had almost not slept last night because he was looking forward to his birthday. It was the first time in a long time that he had not had dreams about his mother.

After school has ended it swarmed in with kids, and Mike was loaded with gifts. He got: Games for the computer, CDs, and a lot of money. The afternoon wefine, though his grandmother thought they were too noisy. Mike did not agree. His grandmother was old that was probably why she was so delicate.

At one point, said one of the girls that she was fed up with her mother that she barely had to keep going. It knew how Mike is not a word. How could one speak of his mother in this way? She should at all be glad that she even had a mother.

Majken had given him a bracelet with his name "Mike" engraved. He was jubilant, and although there had been much to celebrate him, he was constantly not more than ten steps fr Majken. When all the guests had left, was at almost half past eight and Mike was good tender. However, he did not go to bed yet. He was right in and try the new computer, which he had received from his father.

Time flew so exciting was the game. Mike heard not his father entered the room.

- Listen again young man, do not go to bed? It is almost ten ... you can run it tomorrow. Mike closed the game down, brushed his teeth, and soon he lay in his bed but head full of strange ideas about gifts, mothers and birthdays. Dreams of his mother was becoming increasingly been replaced by dreams of Majken.

Chapter 14
Infatuation

Mike had, as the days went on, had many conversations with Majken and he had fallen in love with her. He was also beginning to follow the lessons better … and smile again.

Now and then he had a guilty conscience. Do you have the right to be happy when your mother is dead, what would she say observing from her place in heaven? He should remember to ask her grandmother for advice she was so wise and all-knowing. He had asked Majken for advice and she had agreed that it was okay to be happy. One could not walk around and be sad his or her whole life. Mike has also one day told her of his love for her, and to

his great joy, she felt the same. They had even talked about the possibility of her mother and his father also had to be in love, so they could live together in one big family. They wondered, though, whether it was

possible to be lovers. If their parents were married, they

were the almost brother and sister, and brothers and sisters could not be lovers.

Six months had passed since Mike's mother died. Summer break was soon over, and he was going to school again in about a week. This year, they had not been in Tivoli, which they used to be each summer. Mike had told his father that he would not walk arround in Tivoli, as it guaranteed would not be as much fun as when his mom was alive. His father had muttered something about that life should go on and that time heals all wounds. Mike did not mean that he missed his mother less than he did five months ago. But perhaps his father still had got a point. It wasn't nearly so bad to think of her as it used to be. His nightmares were also gone. Now he dreamed only pleasant dreams, where he sat with his mother in the kitchen and played cards or ate freshly baked buns.

Nadine had become so skilled that she could be stumbling around the house, and say a lot of short words. Mike loved his little sister; but he was still annoyed at her every time she rummaged in his cases.

When he was outside playing or on the way over to Frank, he went often with his head bowed and looked up in the air. There he saw and was small talking with his mother in heaven, while he told her about the things that had happened since he had last spoken to her. Sometimes, if he was busy, he was content just to say "Hi."

Chapter 15
New Years Eve

More than three years have passed by. Majken and Mike was a close-knit couple, who were together as much as possible.

During that time Mike had become almost 14 years old, and Majken had just turned 15. She was a little lady, and Mike loved her more than anything on earth.

It was New Years Eve. It had snowed since Christmas Eve. They had decided to go to the churchyard before they were celebrating New Years Eve at home with Majkens mother. Mike's father also came to the party. He had for almost two years been a friend of Majkens mother who had brought him "back" to normal life.

They were 14 people, and Majkens mother had made seafood mix in a sweet chili sauce on salad with baguettes, roast beef tenderloin and ice cream with fruit for dessert.

They were first past Mike's mother's grave. On the tombstone you could discern the golden letters "Loved and missed" in the middle of the blanket of snow. They had bought two wreaths. Mike put one on his mother's grave. The words were eternal; but the saying "Time heals all wounds" had a grain of truth. He missed his mother still; but it did not hurt his soul anymore.

After about five miutes walk they got to Majken's Dad's grave. It was a magnificent tomb with many evergreen shrubs and small pebbles scattered between stepping stones and shrubs.

Majken leaned against the railing that surrounded her

father's snow-covered grave. Mike seems she looked like a million, as she stood there in her new red dress.
Mike sat on a bench a few feet away.
- Don't you freeze ... you have goose bumps on your arms?

Majken shook her head.
- No! But let's go back to the taxi.
She went to Mike, bent slightly forward and kissed him.
A feeling of happiness flowed through his body. He watched one cumulus cloud that drifted by in the air, which looked threatening ready for a new snowfall. In a split second he thinks he saw his mother sitting in the cloud, and

she gave him thumbs up. He got up from the bench and put his arm around Majken shoulder. There was not a shadow of a doubt in his mind that she would have loved Majken. Mike grabbed the cardoor handles.
- Ladies first

Chapter 16
Mike's stepmom

One day after school Mike could feel that his father was different than he used to be. At dinner time he finally found the words.

- Mike ... there's something I want to tell you. You know how much I loved your mother, and how much I still miss her. But life gotta move on, as I have said before. So I have found a girlfriend who works inside the company. She is very cute ... I think you'll like her right away ... she is paying us a visit tonight. I hope that the two of you just become good friends, then much has been achieved ... I know not whether something will come between Lisa and me, yes by the way her name is Lisa ... but I do not want to live alone any more without a woman I can love. I hope that you will give her a chance. Mike looked at his father.

- I fully understand that you want a life with a new woman. Mother believes guaranteed the same up in her heaven ... I myself am deliriously happy with Majken. I'll soon move to Copenhagen to study at the university ... You have soon lived nine years in cøliat. It's an incredibly long period of time ... so go ahead let the horses loose.

- I am glad that you are so positive. I know that I should not ask you for permission; but it is very important to me that you and she have a chemistry that fit together.

- If you like her father, then I guaranteed do.

The time was seven when the doorbell rang. Mike's father rushed out to open, and Mike could hear that he greeted warmly Lisa. They came into the room, and Mike had to admit that she was a very nice woman, not as nice as his mother but almost. She had long brown hair, and when she greeted him, he sensed a wonderful fragrance, which probably came from her perfume.
- Mike I presume? ... A nice young man ... You must excuse my bad manners, My name is Lisa.
She reached out, and Mike immediately noticed the solid handshake. Additionally, he fell instantly for her winning smile.

After six months' acquaintance she moved into the house, and Mike seemed more and more that she belonged. She was not so good at baking, as his mother had been; but she had teamed up with his grandmother, who promised that Lisa would soon be "trained" as a baker.

When Lisa had lived in the house with his father and Nadine for almost a year, they were married. His father would really have been satisfied with getting married at the City Hall; but when Lisa wants a church wedding, so it must be.

Mike kissed Majken on her mouth.

- It was not your mom …Lisa came along.
Majken took his hand as they walked out of the church. She laughed.
- You can't win it all.